if dogs run free

BOB DYLAN
PICTURES BY SCOTT CAMPBELL

Atheneum Books for Young Readers
NEW YORK LONDON TORONTO SYDNEY NEW DELHI

athenium

ATHENEUM BOOKS FOR YOUNG READERS
An imprint of Simon & Schuster Children's Publishing Division
1230 Avenue of the Americas, New York, New York 10020
Text copyright © 1970 by Big Sky Music; copyright renewed © 1998 by Big Sky Music
Illustrations copyright © 2013 by Scott Campbell
ATHENEUM BOOKS FOR YOUNG READERS is a registered trademark of Simon & Schuster, Inc.
Atheneum logo is a trademark of Simon & Schuster, Inc.
For information about special discounts for bulk purchases, please contact Simon & Schuster Special Sales at
1-866-506-1949 or business@simonandschuster.com.
The Simon & Schuster Speakers Bureau can bring authors to your live event. For more information or to book
an event, contact the Simon & Schuster Speakers Bureau at 1-866-248-3049 or visit our website at
www.simonspeakers.com.
Book design by Sonia Chaghatzbanian
The text for this book is set in Abadi MT.
The illustrations for this book are rendered in watercolor.
Manufactured in China
0613 SCP
First Edition
2 4 6 8 10 9 7 5 3 1
Library of Congress Cataloging-in-Publication Data
Dylan, Bob, 1941–
If dogs run free / Bob Dylan ; illustrated by Scott Campbell. — 1st ed.
p. cm.
Summary: An illustrated version of the Bob Dylan song that asks the question "If dogs run free, why not we?"
ISBN 978-1-4516-4879-9 (hardcover)
ISBN 978-1-4516-4880-5 (eBook)
1. Children's songs, English—United States—Texts. [1. Songs.] I. Campbell, Scott, 1973– ill. II. Title.
PZ8.3.D985If 2013
782.42—dc23
[E]   2012004224

For Grandpa and Grandma Aiken and Grandpa and Grandma Campbell
—S. C.

If dogs run free, then why not we
Across the swooping plain?

My ears hear a symphony
Of two mules, trains, and rain.

The best is always yet to come,

That's what they explain to me.

Just do your thing,

you'll be king

If dogs run free.

My mind weaves a symphony
And tapestry of rhyme.

Oh, winds which rush my tale to thee

So it may flow and be.

To each his own,

it's all unknown

If dogs run free.

If dogs run free, then what must be

Must be,
and that is all.

True love can make a blade of grass

Stand up straight and tall.

In harmony with the cosmic sea

True love needs no company.

It can cure the soul, it can make it whole,

If dogs run free.